For Nancy-Clare, who knew that
make-believe has no boundaries —L.L.

For Christopher Dooley —M.J.

Text copyright © 2010 by Lyn Loates
Illustrations copyright © 2010 by Mark Jones
All rights reserved / CIP Data is available.
Published in the United States 2010 by
🍎 Blue Apple Books
515 Valley Street, Maplewood, NJ 07040
www.blueapplebooks.com
First Edition   Printed in China 09/10
ISBN: 978-1-60905-049-8
1 2 3 4 5 6 7 8 9 10

Distributed in the U.S. by Chronicle Books

CHRISTMAS DELICIOUS

by Lyn Loates • illustrations by Mark Jones

ZANZIBAR'S
DELI

● BLUE APPLE BOOKS

Raisin and Rice, two satisfied mice,
　E-nooormously fat 'round the belly,
Nibbled and chewed on the very best food
　In the storeroom of Zanzibar's Deli.

On Zanzibar's shelves they'd made for themselves
A home on Shelf One-Sixty-Four,
Amidst the fine smell their noses knew well
Of the food they had come to adore.

Where they once lived before,
they were hungry and poor,
With hardly enough food to eat.
But now they had lamb
and hot dogs and ham—
Every day a delicious new treat.

One day Raisin said,
"I've been thinking ahead.
Christmas is not far away.
How nice it would be
to put up a tree
And have a fine feast
Christmas Day."

"Our party could start
with a nice custard tart
Covered in raspberry jelly,
Striped ribbon candy—
now that would be dandy—
And the best pumpkin pie
in the deli.

Cookies and cake.
What else should we make?
Gingerbread men, I would say.
A lovely roast goose,
rich chocolate mousse,
And ice cream
to top off the day!"

"Although it sounds nice,"
said Raisin to Rice,
"This menu is very ambitious."
"Don't worry," Rice cried.
"We'll work side by side
And make our
Christmas delicious!"

"Since there's so much to do,
for me and for you,"
said Raisin who wanted things right.
"I must insist we make out a list
And check it each day and each night."

In the deli that night,
the two were a sight,
Mixing sugar and eggs and yeast.
Brewing and baking
and stewing and shaking,
In the end they had cooked quite a feast.

Then they cleaned and they scrubbed, polished and rubbed,
With mop, dust rag, and broom.
Finally with glee, they trimmed a huge tree
That was *much* too big for the room.

When all had been done for the holiday fun,
They climbed to Shelf One-Sixty-Four
And slept through the night until it was light,
When Raisin peeked out the front door.

A fresh fallen snow
made Zanzibar's glow
Like a jewel
on a bed of soft fleece.
Not a peep, not a sound,
no one rushing around.
On this Christmas Day,
there was peace.

"Christmas is here!
Good health and good cheer!"
said Rice. "It's my favorite day."
"We're up with the sun.
It's time to have fun."
But Raisin had something to say.

"We've plenty of cakes, the cookies are baked,
And more than enough apple pie.
It's all a delight, but something's not right."
Then Rice let out a loud cry!

"With goodies galore,
how did we ignore
What should be at the
top of the list?
Not ice cream. Not custard.
Not sausage or mustard.
It's all of our *friends*
that we missed!"

"As quick as we can, let's think up a plan
To invite all the friends that we know.
We'll ring and we'll knock at each door on the block.
Let's hope everybody will show."

By the time they got home,
they were chilled to the bone.
Then Raisin looked up at the clock.
"I'm feeling quite glum.
It's so late; will they come?"
And that's when the mice heard,
KNOCK-KNOCK!

There were their guests, dressed in their best,
Lined up in a lively procession.
By foot and on sleigh, they'd all made their way
To the Zanzibar Delicatessen.

"We're so glad you've come.
We hope you have fun.
And eat 'til you burst at the seams.
It's such a delight that you're here tonight
to share in our Christmas dreams."

The dances and songs went on all night long,
'Til the stars disappeared from the sky.
When the party was done, friends left one by one,
Saying, "Thanks, goodnight and goodbye."

Raisin and Rice,
two sleepy mice,
Were sure that they'd
never forget . . .
The guests! The food!
The warm holiday mood!
This was their best
Christmas yet.

Now you can tell
why their plan turned out well.
The mice showed their friends
that they cared.
They both learned anew
what has always been true:

Christmas is best when it's shared!

Raisin and Rice Christmas Treats

INGREDIENTS

¼ cup unsalted butter
2 cups marshmallows
½ cup milk-chocolate chips
4 cups puffed or crispy rice cereal
¾ cup raisins

DIRECTIONS

Line a 9" x 9" baking pan with parchment paper so that the Christmas Treats don't stick to the pan.

In a large non-stick pot, first melt butter on low heat. Then add marshmallows and milk-chocolate chips. Use a spatula to stir until all ingredients are well combined.

Next, add puffed or crispy rice cereal and raisins. Stir together until well coated.

Using a spatula, quickly spoon the mixture into the baking pan. Spread until evenly distributed. If mixture sticks, coat the spatula with either butter or non-stick cooking spray. Press the mixture down with spatula until it's flat.

Cool for 15-20 minutes.

Carefully remove the Christmas Treats from pan by lifting out parchment paper. Cut into 2" x 2" squares.

A grown-up must help a child with this recipe.